Front endpapers by Amber Parker aged 7
Back endpapers by Maggie Thomas aged 7
Thank you to Star of the Sea RC Primary School, Whitley Bay
for helping with the endpapers – K.P.

For Margaret Shewan, to celebrate her 70th birthday – V.T.
For Helen Mortimer – K.P.

# OXFORD
## UNIVERSITY PRESS

Great Clarendon Street, Oxford OX2 6DP

Oxford University Press is a department of the University of Oxford.
It furthers the University's objective of excellence in research, scholarship,
and education by publishing worldwide in

Oxford  New York

Auckland  Cape Town  Dar es Salaam  Hong Kong  Karachi
Kuala Lumpur  Madrid  Melbourne  Mexico City  Nairobi
New Delhi  Shanghai  Taipei  Toronto

With offices in

Argentina  Austria  Brazil  Chile  Czech Republic  France  Greece
Guatemala  Hungary  Italy  Japan  Poland  Portugal  Singapore
South Korea  Switzerland  Thailand  Turkey  Ukraine  Vietnam

Oxford is a registered trade mark of Oxford University Press
in the UK and in certain other countries

British Library Cataloguing in Publication Data available

ISBN: 978-0-19-272908-8 (hardback)

Printed in Singapore

Paper used in the production of this book is a natural, recyclable product made
from wood grown in sustainable forests. The manufacturing process conforms to the
environmental regulations of the country of origin

www.korkypaul.com

Valerie Thomas and Korky Paul

# Winnie's
## Amazing Pumpkin

OXFORD
UNIVERSITY PRESS

Winnie the Witch ate lots of vegetables.

She liked broccoli, cauliflower,
cabbage, and parsnips.
She really liked peas, carrots,
beans, potatoes, and spinach.

But she *loved* pumpkin.
She loved pumpkin soup, pumpkin pie, and
pumpkin scones with pumpkin seeds on top.
But, most of all, she loved roast pumpkin.

Wilbur, her big black cat,
liked pumpkin soup if it
had lots of cream stirred in.

Every Saturday morning Winnie would jump onto her broomstick, Wilbur would jump onto her shoulder, and they would zoom off to the farmers' market to buy their vegetables.

That was easy.

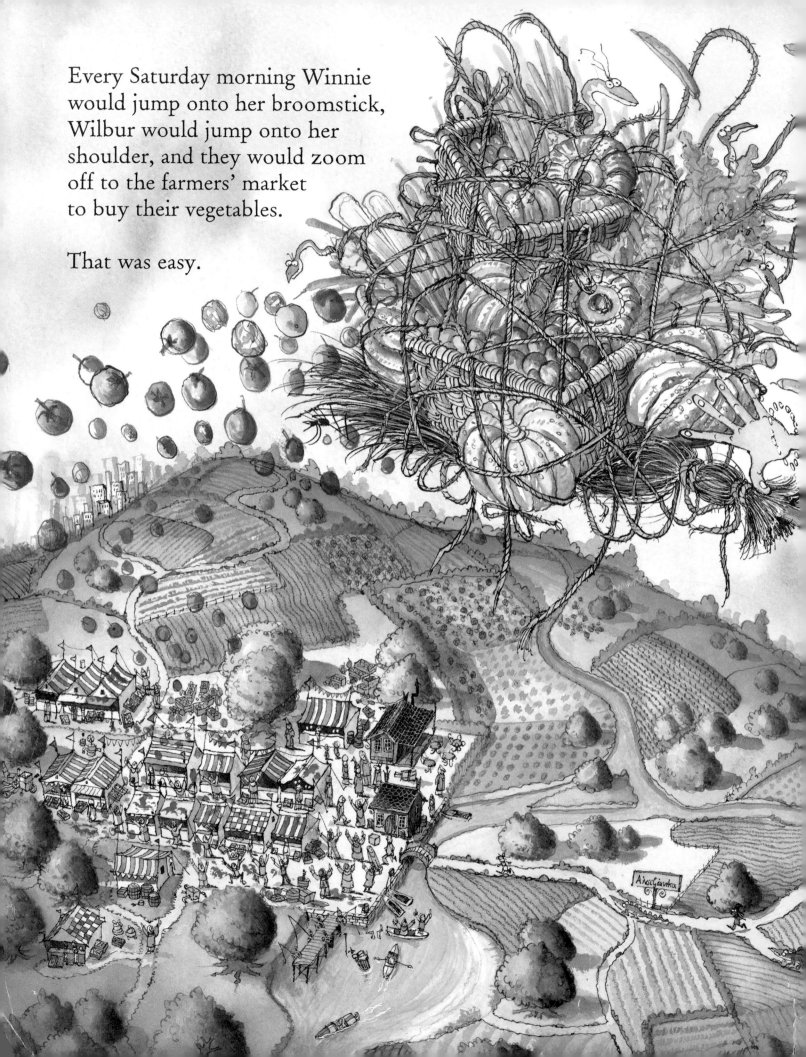

But it wasn't so easy coming home.
It is hard to balance on a broomstick with
a cat, pumpkins, and lots of other vegetables.

**Ooops!** Brussels sprouts and tomatoes
rained down on the market.

**Splat! Squelch!**

'Blithering broomsticks!' shouted Winnie.
And then she had a good idea.

'I'll grow my own vegetables,' she said.
So Winnie dug a big vegetable patch
in her garden.

Wilbur helped.

She planted lots and lots of vegetables.
She watered the plants and pulled up
the weeds.

Wilbur helped.

But the plants grew very slowly.

And, when they did grow, the caterpillars
and snails and rabbits ate them.

'Oh dear,' said Winnie. 'Gardening is hard work.
I'll try a spell to help my garden grow.'

She waved her magic wand, shouted,

Abracadabra!

and nothing happened.

'Bother!' said Winnie. 'That didn't work. I'll go and look in my Big Book of Spells.'

Winnie went inside just a minute too soon.

Outside, the spell began to work.

Inside, it was very dark.
Winnie tripped over Wilbur.

**'Meooowww!'**
'I'm sorry, Wilbur,' said Winnie,
'I didn't see you. It's so dark, there
must be a storm on the way.'

She looked out of the window.
It wasn't a storm.
It was Winnie's garden.
The vegetables were growing so fast
they covered all the windows.

'I'd better go out and stop
the spell,' Winnie said.

But the door wouldn't open.
An enormous cabbage was in the way.

Winnie rushed upstairs, climbed
out of the bathroom window,
and slid down a giant beanstalk.

Wilbur climbed down behind her.
'This is fun!' he thought,
until he met a giant caterpillar.

**'Yeeoow!'**

Everything in Winnie's garden was
enormous, gigantic, stupendous!

A beanstalk was growing up into the clouds.
The cabbages were as big as cows.
The rabbits were bigger than cows.
An immense pumpkin vine was curling
around Winnie's house.

And there, on the roof, was a **huge** pumpkin.
'Oh no!' shouted Winnie.
'The pumpkin will squash my house!'
She waved her magic wand,
but just as she shouted . . .

Abra . . . .

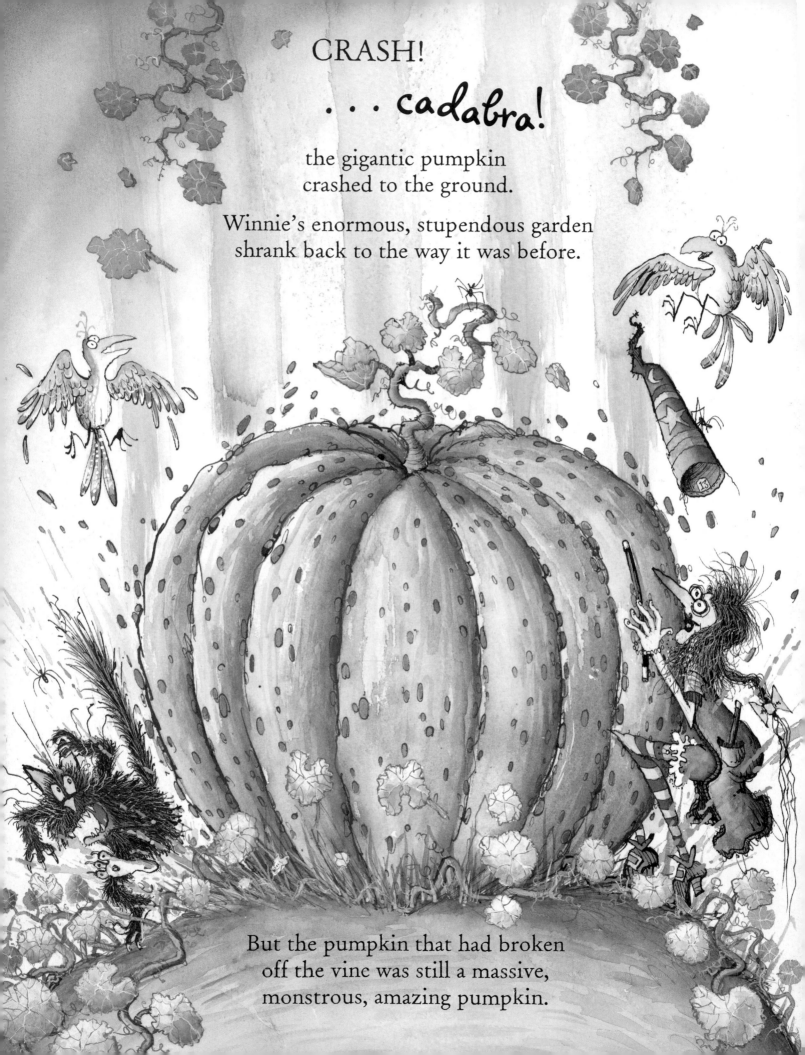

CRASH!

. . . cadabra!

the gigantic pumpkin
crashed to the ground.

Winnie's enormous, stupendous garden
shrank back to the way it was before.

But the pumpkin that had broken
off the vine was still a massive,
monstrous, amazing pumpkin.

Winnie chopped a doorway into the pumpkin.

She made pumpkin pies, pumpkin scones, pumpkin soup with cream for Wilbur, and an enormous dish of roast pumpkin.

But there was still lots of pumpkin left.

So she put a notice on the gate:

★FREE★
PUMPKIN
★
Help yourself...

People came with their bowls and
baskets and even wheelbarrows.

And soon the pumpkin shell was empty.

'What shall I do with the pumpkin shell?' wondered Winnie.
'It would make a good house, but I already have a house.

One of my friends once changed a pumpkin into a coach.
But that was for a special occasion.
And the horses might be a problem.'

Then Winnie had a wonderful idea.
'Yes!' she said. 'That's exactly what
it looks like,' she said. 'Of course!'

She waved her magic wand,
stamped her foot, shouted,

Abracadabra!

and there, in Winnie's garden,
was a bright orange helicopter.

So now, when Winnie and Wilbur go to the market, Winnie can buy as many pumpkins as she likes.

And flying home in a helicopter is lots of fun!